IT'S A GOOD THING

STORY BY JOAN BUCHANAN

PICTURES BY BARBARA DI LELLA

Annick Press

Second printing, May 1985

Annick Press Ltd.

Annick Press gratefully acknowleges
the support of The Canada Council and
The Ontario Arts Council

Design and graphic realization: Barbara DiLella

Canadian Cataloguing in Publication Data

Buchanan, Joan.
  It's a good thing

ISBN 0-920236-72-3 (bound). — ISBN 0-920236-65-0 (pbk.)

I. DiLella, Barbara.   II. Title.

PS8553.U23I77 1983   jC813'.54   C84-098105-8
PZ7.B83It 1983

Distributed in Canada and the USA by:
Firefly Books Ltd.
3520 Pharmacy Avenue, Unit 1c
Scarborough, Ontario
M1W 2T8

Printed and bound in Canada by
D.W. Friesen & Sons Ltd.

IT WAS COLD OUT.
Marie looked up at the clouds in the sky.
"Those clouds look just like cotton candy," Marie began to daydream.
"If I were a GIANT,
I'd eat cotton candy for breakfast. I'd tear off little pieces to give to my friends."

For Heather

DOWN,
DOWN,
Down
the
hill
to the beach went Marie
and her little sister Elizabeth.

Marie was taking Elizabeth for a walk. She had to be careful. She was in charge. She wasn't supposed to daydream.

SHE wasn't hurt.
And rolling was fun,
so Marie kept on rolling
down,
Down,
DOWN the hill,
just like a piece of cotton fluff in the wind.

"WATCH OUT

STOP!
YOU'LL HIT A STUMP!"
shouted Elizabeth.

"IT'S A GOOD THING
you saved me,
or else
there wouldn't be anyone
to look after you,"
said Marie.
"Hmm..." Elizabeth said.

MARIE didn't see the
loose stones in front of her.
Elizabeth did and walked carefully
around them, down the path. But   O   O   P   S !
        Marie stumbled and rolled
                        and Rolled
                                and ROLLED
        down   the   path.

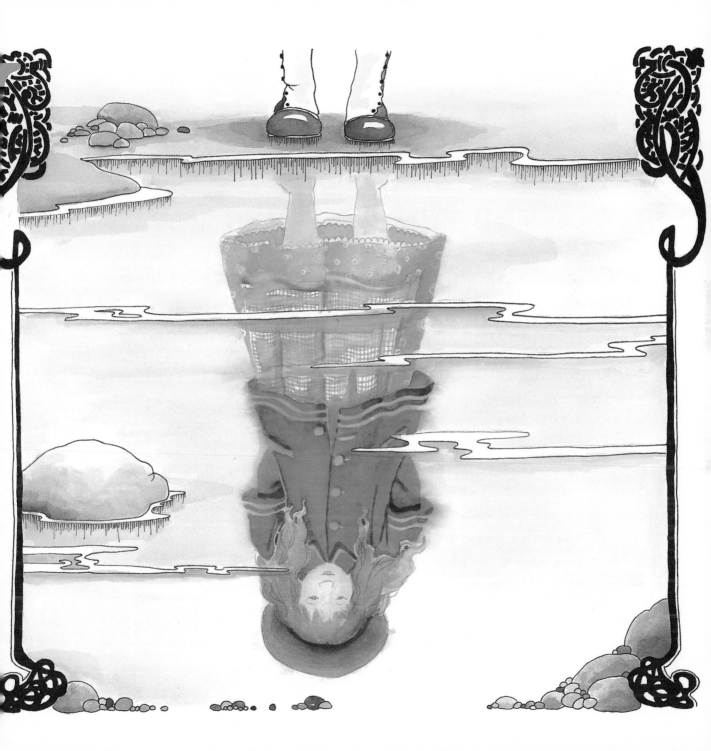

"HURRY, MARIE!
RUN!
THE TIDE IS COMING IN!"
shouted Elizabeth.

The tide was coming in fast. Marie looked down at her feet. The water was touching her toes. It was nearly winter and the water was very cold. Soon it would be at her ankles. Marie jumped back quickly and ran to her sister on dry land.

THEN MARIE AND ELIZABETH reached the beach and the sand. The tide was out. They could see their reflections in the tidepools.

"If I were a GIANT, I'd take my baths in the sea, and use sailing ships for toys," thought Marie. "People would go hiking on my nose and slide down my arm into the water..."

MARIE climbed onto a large rock.
She began to flap her arms very hard.
"See, I can fly like a bird!"
she said to Elizabeth.

IT'S A GOOD THING
you saved me, or else
there wouldn't be anyone
to look after you,"
said Marie.
"Hmm..." said Elizabeth.
"Let's walk in the forest. It's safer," Elizabeth said.

SO ELIZABETH AND MARIE
walked on the forest path above the beach.
"Yes, this is a better idea," said Marie.
"And safer. Look at all the geese flying south
for the winter!"
Elizabeth and Marie looked up.

SOON THEY came to a stream.
"Okay, Elizabeth. I'll help you get
across," said Marie.
"No. I can get across by myself. All
you can do is daydream," Elizabeth said.
Elizabeth jumped on a stone then to a log.
"WAIT, Elizabeth! That doesn't
look very safe!" called Marie.

All of a sudden, the log S A N K.
Elizabeth sank too.
She fell in the cold, C O L D water right up to her
hips. Marie tugged her out as quick as a wink and
grabbed her little sister's hand and ran
and R A N
and R A N
along the forest path, along the beach and up the hill:
home.

She pretended she was a bird.
"I am a GIANT BIRD.
I'm flying to the moon to pick up rocks for my collection," she thought.
Marie jumped.

"LOOK OUT!

YOU'LL LAND IN THAT BIG HOLE!"

shouted Elizabeth.

Marie twisted to the side. She just missed the
big hole.

"IT'S A GOOD THING
you saved me,
or else
there wouldn't be anyone
to look after you,"
said Marie.
"Hmm…" Elizabeth said.

"IT'S A GOOD THING

you saved me, or else
there wouldn't be anyone
to look after you," said Elizabeth.
"Hmm…" said Marie.

RIGHT AWAY Marie took off Elizabeth's wet clothes, and put her in a hot bath, and dried her off, and bundled her in blankets by the fire, and gave her hot tea with lots of cream and sugar.